D0852831

Be Brave,
Morgan!

Morgan's Got Game

Morgan's Got

by Ted Staunton

illustrated by Bill Slavin

Game

Formac Publishing Company Limited
Halifax

Formac Publishing Company Limited recognizes the support of the Province of
Nova Scotia through the Department of Communities, Culture and Heritage.
We are pleased to work in partnership with the Province of Nova Scotia
to develop and promote our cultural resources for all Nova Scotians. We
acknowledge the support of the Canada Council for the Arts, which last year
invested $153 million to bring the arts to Canadians throughout the country.
This project has been made possible in part by the Government of Canada.

Cover design: Tyler Cleroux
Cover image: Bill Slavin

Library and Archives Canada Cataloguing in Publication

Staunton, Ted, 1956-, author
        Morgan's got game / Ted Staunton ; illustrated by Bill Slavin.

(Be brave, Morgan!)
Reprint. Originally published: Halifax : Formac Publishing
        Company Limited, 2014.
ISBN 978-1-4595-0508-7 (hardcover)

        I. Slavin, Bill, illustrator II. Title. III. Series: Staunton, Ted,
1956- . Be brave, Morgan!

PS8587.T334M6726 2017   jC813'.54   C2017-905334-5

Published by:
Formac Publishing
Company Limited
5502 Atlantic Street
Halifax, Nova Scotia,
Canada, B3H 1G4
www.formac.ca

Distributed in Canada by:
Formac Lorimer Books
5502 Atlantic Street
Halifax, NS, Canada
B3H 1G4

Distributed in the US by:
Lerner Publisher Services
1251 Washington Ave. N.
Minneapolis, MN, USA
55401
www.lernerbooks.com

Printed and bound in Canada.

Manufactured by Friesens Corporation in Altona, Manitoba,
Canada in August 2017.

Job #236687

Contents

Chapter One

Outside Looking In

It's recess. I'm in the school yard with my nose pressed against the library window. Behind me,
everyone is running and yelling.
I don't care about that. I have

my soccer ball under my arm,
but I don't care about that
either.

The glass is cold against my
nose. My breath clouds up the
window but I can still see inside.
Kids are sitting in comfy chairs
with their Robogamer Z7s.
My best friend Charlie is in
there. His Z7 is hooked up to
Curtis's. Charlie and I don't
even like Curtis.

I bet they're playing
Dragon's Gold.

I can't play *Dragon's Gold*
unless I'm on my game console
at home. Guess who doesn't
have a cool Robogamer Z7 so

he can play at school? Guess whose mom and dad said no?

Guess who is the poorest, saddest kid in the whole world?

It's so not-fair I could almost cry.

In fact I'm starting to sniffle when — *WHUMPF* — somebody punches the soccer ball out from under my arm. It bounces off the wall under the window. My forehead bonks the glass.

"Ow!"

Inside, no one even looks up from their Z7. I spin around. Aldeen Hummel, the Godzilla of Grade Three, is running away with my ball. Her witchy hair bobs like bumblebees around her head. "Use it or lose it, bozo!" she yells.

Now I'm supposed to chase Aldeen. She does this every recess when I stare in the window. She calls it soccer tag. I call it yucky.

I hate chasing Aldeen.

I never catch her.

And if I ever did catch her, she'd probably give me a killer noogie. Chasing Aldeen is like chasing the sneaky elves in *Dragon's Gold* — they always zap you too. The difference

is, I don't get out of breath
tapping my game controller.

I watch Aldeen race to the
top of the adventure climber.
She sticks her tongue out at
me.

"Come on, Morgan. Or I win!"

Did I mention that if I don't try
I get a killer noogie anyway? I
start to run.

Chapter Two

Bubblegum Swamp

After school, Aldeen, Charlie, and I go to my place to play *Dragon's Gold*. Aldeen gets to come to my house when her mom and her Granny Flo are both working.

She still has my soccer ball.

She's bouncing it like a
basketball, but with her fist.

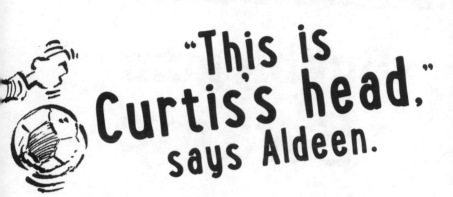

"This is
Curtis's head,"
says Aldeen.

She doesn't like Curtis either.
There are lots of people
Godzilla doesn't like.

"We had a great soccer
game at recess," I lie to
Charlie. Charlie loves soccer.
Maybe tomorrow he'll want
to come outside and play. All
Charlie says is, "Curtis tricked

me when I got to the fourth level. He flushed me back to the bubblegum swamp in level one."

"That's easy to get out of," Aldeen says. "I'll show you at Morgan's." Bonk, bonk, bonk goes the ball.

Dad is home. He gives us

juice and cookies. I hook up the game controllers. Sure enough, Aldeen shows Charlie a cheat that makes the dragon blow

a **GIANT** gum bubble

that lifts you all the way to
level three. "Cool," I say.
Aldeen shrugs.

She's really good at Dragon's
Gold.

It's the only game she has
at her house. I once heard
my mom say Aldeen's family
doesn't have much money.

Charlie gets out his Z7 and tries the cheat on it. It works. Dad comes in. "So, this is the fabled Z7," he says.

"Please, can I get one?" I ask for the millionth time. "Everyone has one."

"Everyone?"

Dad smiles.

"Almost," I say.

"I'm getting one," Aldeen nods, "from my Gran. Any day now."

"That's nice," Dad says. "We'll see, kiddo. Right now, everyone go outside. It's too nice to stay indoors staring at a screen."

I groan. "Can we have another cookie first?"

"You'll spoil your dinner." I have a tough dad.

Outside, Aldeen runs away for soccer tag again. Not even Charlie can catch her.
When we finally give up I pant to her, "Are you . . . really . . . getting . . . a Z7?"

Aldeen nods. She's not panting. "Any day now."

It's time for me to get one too.

Chapter Three

Sticker
Shock

Next morning, I walk to school
with Charlie. Curtis and his dad
drive past in their Hummer.
Curtis waves as if he's king or
something.

When we get to school,
Curtis is pretend-showing

Bobby how he can smash a
board with one karate chop.

"My dad can smash
bricks," Curtis says.

"He's
Superman."

Then he sees us. "Hey, Charlie,
still stuck in bubblegum?"

"Nope," Charlie says. "I got
the dragon to blow a bubble
and now I'm back in level
three. Aldeen showed me."

Curtis rolls his eyes. "Man,

that cheat's as old as the hills.
I could show you one that
sends you to level eight. But
I'll probably squish you down
to level one first."

"Yeah, right, Curtis," I say.
"Have you even got to level
eight?"

"Ages ago, Morgan. You
might get there too — with a
talent transplant and a Z7."

There is no way Curtis is at
level eight.

What a liar!

I start to say, "Yeah, well at
home I'm at —" when Aldeen

walks by very slowly. Aldeen
never does anything slowly.
She's not looking at us either,
she's staring at something in her
hands. Her thumbs are bopping.

Aldeen Hummel has a Robogamer Z7.

"Hey," I say, "let's see."

"Buzz off. I'm busy." Aldeen
doesn't look up.

"They're hard to see outside,
huh?" Charlie says.

"Mine has a special screen,"
Aldeen says. She keeps
moving.

"The Glare Guard," says
Curtis, who knows everything.
He has a Z7 too.

"Can I look?" Bobby says.

"I said, I'm busy."

Aldeen's thumbs keep moving.

The bell rings. Aldeen shoves her Z7 in her backpack as we line up.

"Don't forget to power off,"

Charlie says to her. Aldeen's eyes squinch up behind her glasses. Then she reaches in the pack and feels for the power button.

In class I watch Aldeen show our teacher, Mrs. Ross, her Z7. On the wall hangs this big cloth thing with pockets in it, like my mom has for shoes.

Everybody who has a phone or a game player gets their own pocket to keep it in.
I watch Aldeen get a name sticker. She goes over to the cloth thing and picks a pocket. She sticks on her sticker and puts her Z7 inside. At recess she goes to the library with the others. I don't even look in the window.

Aldeen Hummel has a Z7 and I don't.

Chapter Four

Cookies for Cool

I beg Mom and Dad for three days. Well, I don't always beg. Sometimes I just make my eyes go big and sad. Once I sit on the couch and

sniffle.

Mom says to stop whining.
Dad says sulking won't help.
I switch to promising things
instead. I promise to help
rake leaves. I promise to
clear the table every night,
eat vegetables without
complaining, and

give up
cookies.

That last one really gets them.
"Give up cookies?" Mom stares.
　"For a million years," I say.
　"Let's start with a month."
　"Does that mean I get —"
　"We'll see."
　Dirty rat Aldeen won't even
let me look at her Z7, but on
Saturday Dad and I go and get
me my own.

"It's an early Christmas present,"

Dad says.

"I'll remind you Christmas morning. In the meantime, enjoy your veggies."

Monday morning I take my Z7 to school. "Just be careful," Mom warns, "If you lose it or break it, you're out of luck. No loaning, no trading, no sharing.

Those things are expensive."

"I'll put in a password," I say. "Then no one else can use it."

"Uh-uh," Mom says. "You might forget the password too. Then you'd really be out of luck."

It doesn't matter — I'll be super careful. Nothing will happen to my Z7. It is so cool.

I feel so cool.

When we go in at the bell, I get to show Mrs. Ross. I know the other kids are watching as I get my name sticker and go

to the cloth pockets hanging
by the bulletin board. I choose
the pocket beside Charlie's
and above Aldeen's. Now my
name is up there too. I tuck in
my Z7.

At snack time,

I've got broccoli trees.

Oh, well, it's worth it. Now
I get to go to the library.
There's me, Charlie, Ian, Mark,
Kaely, Aldeen — and Curtis. As
we head to the library, Curtis
looks at me and sighs as if he's
super bored.

"Well, looks as if

I'll have to zap another loser

at *Dragon's Gold*."

"I'm playing with Charlie," I say.

"Guess you're chicken, then," says Curtis. "Like Aldeen. Maybe she's your girlfriend."

I play with Curtis.

Chapter Five

Out

I don't like playing with Curtis. Nobody likes playing with Curtis. He doesn't cheat, exactly,

but he'll do anything to mess you up.

I land in the bubblegum swamp
three times in two days.

Meanwhile, Ian and Charlie
are partnered up in their own
game, and so are Mark and
Kaely. I ask Aldeen if I can
play with her instead.

"No way, José,"

she says.

"But we can just hook up our
Z7s," I say, "like we play on
my TV after school."

"That's different."

"How?"

"It just is."

"But now I have to play with
Curtis all the time. It's no fair."

Aldeen stares at me. Then

she says, "Tough noogies."

Aldeen won't play with anyone else, either. She won't even show what game she's playing. When we get to the library she just races to the bathtub filled with cushions, hops in and bops away with her thumbs. She looks like a crazy submarine driver or something. And that means

I'm stuck,

because nobody else will trade partners.

By Friday, I'm almost wishing I was playing soccer tag again.

When the bell goes, I hurry to
the library and climb in the tub
before Aldeen gets there. She
walks in and sees me. Her eyes
go squinchy.

Up pops her killer
noogie knuckle.

"Out."

"Come on, Aldeen," I beg.
"Play with me just this once."

Aldeen shakes her head. Her
witchy hair bounces. "No. Out."

"Pul-eeze . . ." But it's too
late. Curtis struts in and hears
me.

"Yeah, come on, Aldeen,"

he imitates me.

"Play with your boyfriend."

Kaely laughs.
Oh-oh.
I can feel my face getting red
as the cushions in the tub.

"Aldeen's too

chicken

to play with anybody," Curtis
calls. "She probably can't even
play. She probably doesn't
even have a real Z7. I bet it
doesn't even work!"

Aldeen clutches her Z7 as if
it's a life saver in a swimming
pool. Her face turns as purple
as her sweatsuit.

Smoke is practically coming out her ears.

I figure she's about one second from feeding Curtis his own Z7. Then she turns back to me and says,

"Out."

Chapter Six

Goading Godzilla

It isn't enough that Curtis zaps me playing *Dragon's Gold* again; now he's on a roll about Aldeen. When we head back to class after recess, I stick with Charlie. It's never smart to walk close to Aldeen when

she's in a bad mood. Besides,
I don't want anybody thinking
I'm Aldeen's boyfriend.

Curtis keeps picking on her.
"Hey, Aldeen, is it fun with no
power? I peeked.

There was nothing on your screen!"

I know that's a lie, because
Curtis spent all recess
dumping me in the

bubblegum
swamp.

I don't say that though. I tell
myself it won't help if I call
Curtis a liar, he'd keep on
being a jerk anyway. By the
time we get down the hall,
Curtis has a new name for
Aldeen: "Hey, Aldeen Empty-
Screen!"

It's not like the Gozilla
of Grade Three has lots of

friends, but you can feel kids
starting to wish Curtis would
shut up.

I want Curtis to shut up.
I tell myself it won't help if I
say anything. He'll just say I'm
Aldeen's boyfriend again.

We go into class. When
Aldeen puts her Z7 into its
pocket, Curtis fakes a grab
for it.

Aldeen yells and whips around so fast her glasses almost fly off.

"Ha-ha. Kidding," Curtis smirks.

"Aw, cut it out, Curtis," Charlie puts away his own Z7.

"What, are you her boyfriend too, Charlie?"

Mrs. Ross is walking over to see what's going on. Charlie shakes his head and goes to his desk. Aldeen stays right where she is. She's making a kind of growly sound at Curtis. Curtis laughs at her.

"Right, Aldeen Empty-Screen," he says.

"Don't forget, I know karate." Yeah, I tell myself,

but Aldeen knows wedgies.
It won't help if I say it though; I
just go to my desk.

The rest of the day Curtis keeps bugging Aldeen.

When he goes to sharpen his pencil, he shoots out a hand as he passes the Z7 pockets.

He passes around a crummy
drawing of a Z7 with a
blank screen and the words
ALDEEN'S BRAIN. In the
library at afternoon recess he
doesn't make me play with
him. Instead, we all watch
as he keeps drifting past
the bathtub where Aldeen
is, trying to see her screen.
Aldeen keeps shoving her Z7
under the cushions. Finally, the
librarian tells Curtis he'll have
to go outside if he's not going
to use his Z7 quietly.

He goes all innocent.
"But Aldeen's not even really using hers. It doesn't work. She's just pretending."

"Aldeen is not disturbing anyone. Either do the same or out you go."

When the bell finally goes and Aldeen climbs out of the bathtub, Curtis walks up to her

in front of everyone. "Hey, Empty-Screen. Monday.

You and me play together or you're chicken and everyone will know that thing is junk.

Get a real one if you're not too poor."

Aldeen's knuckles go white around her Z7. I wait for the killer noogie knuckle to pop up, for Godzilla to roar. Godzilla doesn't roar. Aldeen bites down hard on her lips. Curtis laughs and walks away.

Everyone does. I start to walk away too, then look again at Aldeen. Behind her glasses, her eyes are all shiny, as if they're wet with something.

Chapter Seven

Z7
Spy

After school, Aldeen comes
to my house until her Granny
Flo can pick her up. The way
she looks, I'm glad I don't have
my soccer ball. She'd probably
explode it with one punch. All

the way home I wonder if Curtis
is right.

What if Aldeen has been faking?

But why would she have a Z7
that doesn't work? She said her
Granny Flo was getting her one,
right? I tell myself her Z7 has
to work.

Mom has carrot sticks for our
snack. I know better than to
complain. Aldeen crunches them
like a T-Rex munching up Curtis.
But when we go outside for
soccer tag, she barely runs away
from me with the ball. I don't

know what to do when I catch her because I've never caught her before. Inside, she won't even play *Dragon's Gold*.

I want to ask her if Curtis is right. I don't ask. I tell myself that her not giving Curtis a killer wedgie doesn't mean she won't give me one. The doorbell rings. It's Aldeen's Granny Flo. The taxi she drives is parked out front and she smells of her little cigars. "Hiya, Morgan," she crows. "Aldy, time to go!"

"I gotta go to the bathroom first,"

Aldeen says.

"Make it snappy, kiddo." Granny Flo steps in and picks up Aldeen's backpack. "What's heavy?" She opens it and pulls out the Z7.

"Is she still carting this around?"

Mom comes out. Granny Flo puts Aldeen's stuff down and they go in the kitchen. The backpack is still open. There's the Z7. I look down the hall to the bathroom door. It's closed. I grab the Z7 and press the power button. The little light

doesn't pop on. The screen
stays dark. I turn it to look at
the button.

Something rattles inside.
Z7s aren't supposed to rattle.

A flush sounds from the
bathroom. I shove the Z7 into
the backpack, tug the zip
closed, then dive for the living-
room couch. Aldeen comes
down the hall. She looks at her
pack, then at me. "See you,"
I say. I'm still panting a little
from racing around.

Mom and Granny Flo come back. "All set?" Aldeen grabs her backpack. As our door closes behind them, I hear Granny Flo saying "Why are you lugging that old —"

Curtis was right. On Monday, Aldeen is doomed.

Chapter Eight

Sub-Atomic
Wedgie

All weekend I tell myself it
doesn't matter that I didn't call
Curtis a liar. I tell myself he'd
call me Aldeen's boyfriend if
I said anything. I tell myself
Aldeen can give Curtis an atomic
wedgie any time she wants.

I try to tell myself I wasn't being a chicken.

But something reminds me I was wrong about Aldeen's Z7. It tells me Aldeen's not going to be giving any atomic wedgies to Curtis.

The same thing tells me

I *am* a chicken.

It's telling me that, even if Aldeen is the Godzilla of Grade Three, any guy who calls me Godzilla's boyfriend is worse.

Maybe Godzillas need help too.

On Monday I go to school early. I know what I have to do, even if I'm scared to do it. Aldeen is already there. She walks over and puts down her backpack. "Tag," she says, "I'm it."

"I don't want to play," I say.
Up pops her noogie knuckle.
I put down my backpack and
start to run. I don't hear her
chasing me. I look back. She's
still at the backpacks.

"I'm giving you a head start,
doofus," she calls. "You'll need
it." I run again. She catches me
a minute later. I don't catch
her back, but by then it doesn't
matter. Curtis is on top of the
adventure climber, bopping
around and making rapper signs
with his fingers. He chants:

"Al-deen Empty-Screen, gonna whup the Queen of Mean!"

Kids are laughing. Aldeen
doesn't climb up and give
Curtis an atomic wedgie. She
just picks up her backpack and
stands by the door. The bell
rings. I grab my backpack and
wait at the end of the line, just
like I planned. I can use the
rest, too.

And just like I planned,

I'm the last one
to get to our classroom.

It's noisy and busy as I come in. The other Z7s are already hanging up. I hustle over and stand in front of my pocket. Aldeen's is right below mine. No one can see me switch Z7s: mine goes in Aldeen's pocket and hers goes in mine. Mom said no loaning, no trading, no sharing. I'm going to break the rule this once — and Curtis will get a big surprise.

Chapter Nine

Out of the Tub

It takes forever to get to
snacks and recess.
**I have an apple, which is
better than broccoli.**
I munch and whisper to Charlie
how I secretly traded Z7s.

"You'd better tell her," Charlie says. "If she thinks it's hers, she might bash Curtis on the head with it or something, and wreck it."

I never thought of that. When the recess bell goes, I jump up. Curtis grabs his Z7 and races off.

"I'll be waiting,"

he snickers over his shoulder.

Aldeen already has mine. I grab her Z7 from my pocket and hiss, "Don't worry. I swapped with you. Mine works."

Aldeen whips around. She says, "Buzz off."

Then in one laser-fast move she swaps them back and runs.

What the . . . I get mad. Okay, Aldeen, I think, go ahead and lose. I march to the library. Aldeen is across from Curtis. Their Z7s are connected. We all watch as she presses the power button.

Game over,

I think,

but her screen lights up, just
the way it should. *What the .
. .* I look at Charlie. He shrugs.
Curtis looks surprised, but
not as surprised as me, I bet.
"Huh," he says.

Aldeen squinches her eyes.

"Play, bozo."

The librarian makes us all
find our own seats. I climb
in the bathtub and press my
Z7 power button. Nothing
happens. *What the . . .* I
turn it to look at the button.

There's a familiar rattle from inside. Hey . . .

There's nothing for me to do but listen to Curtis groan as Aldeen dumps him in the bubblegum swamp, and wonder how I ended up with Aldeen's Z7 after all.

When we head back after recess, Curtis says, "Who cares about Z7s? My dad is helping me build a go-cart with a real motor."

As he talks, I whisper to Aldeen, "You stole my Z7. Give it back."

We do another fast swap. "You almost wrecked

everything," Aldeen says.

"I did? I was trying to help,
Aldeen, and you took it without
even asking. What'd you do
that for?"

Aldeen doesn't look at me.

""Maybe I didn't think anybody would help.""

I think about being chicken. It doesn't feel good. "Could've asked," I say anyway.

"Could have said," she says back. She goes into class and stuffs her broken Z7 into its pocket.

Chapter Ten

Any Day
Now

Next recess, I go outside. So do Charlie and Aldeen. We play tag with other kids. I even catch Aldeen once, somehow, so I'm not It the whole time.

Maybe that's how Aldeen says thank-you.

When I get home though, I pull out my Z7. I've had enough *Dragon's Gold*, but there's a racing car game I haven't tried yet. Dad says it's good. I finish my celery and peanut butter, wash my hands and power up.

There's a problem:

I can't skip the password screen.

But there isn't a password. Mom told me not to put one in. I try again. My Z7 still asks for the password. *How can there be one if I didn't put one in?* Then my celery and peanut butter do a little flip inside me. Oh . . . no . . . She couldn't have. Could she?

Dad is downstairs. I sneak to the phone and do something I hate doing — I call Aldeen Hummel.

"Whaddya want?" she growls.

"Did you put a password in my Z7?" I hiss.

"Maybe. You should protect your stuff better, so no one can take it and use it."

"Well, what's the word?" I barely keep from shouting.

"I can't use my Z7."

"I'll tell you when I bring mine over. Then we can hook them up and play."

"But yours doesn't even work!"

"Not that one," Aldeen snaps. "That's just a junker someone left in my granny's cab. Two more days till I get my real one."

"Yeah, right," I say. "You said 'any day now' before."

"So? Now it's two days. Someone left a good one in her cab. She always waits ten days before she keeps anything.

There's two days left. Then I'll come over, I'll show you the password and we'll play."

"But what am I gonna do till then?"

"Soccer tag," says Aldeen.

"I'll be right over."

Morgan the Brave

Morgan has to figure out how to go to a birthday party— but avoid seeing the scary movie prom-ised as the main event. Birthday boy Curtis tries to expose anyone missing out on his party as a chicken, so Morgan needs an idea, and quick! Is it possible that Aldeen, Morgan's frenemy who never fails to notice and taunt him about his weaknesses, has the solution? Morgan finds that not everyone is as tough as they look.

Morgan on Ice

Morgan doesn't like to skate, and he's determined not to learn. What he really wants to do is go see Monster Truck-A-Rama with Charlie. Aldeen is not impressed since Morgan already agreed to go to Princesses on Ice with her. Can Morgan keep everyone happy, or is he skating on thin ice?

Daredevil Morgan

Be Brave, Morgan!

Daredevil Morgan

Ted Staunton/Illustrated by Bill Slavin

Morgan's best friend Charlie urges him to try the GraviTwirl ride at the Fall Fair. But Morgan is focused on his homegrown contender for the Perfect Pumpkin contest. That is, until Aldeen Hummel, the Godzilla of Grade Three, drops it!

Morgan faces Aldeen in a bumper car War. Aldeen dares him to go on the Asteroid Belt ride. Will Morgan be brave enough to try? And can he still win the Best Pumpkin Pie contest with the remains of his squished squash?